FLOWER GARDEN

WRITTEN BY

Eve Bunting

ILLUSTRATED BY

Kathryn Hewitt

VOYAGER BOOKS
HARCOURT, INC.
San Diego   New York   London

Requests for permission to make copies of any part of the work
should be mailed to: Permissions Department, Harcourt, Inc.,
6277 Sea Harbor Drive, Orlando, Florida 32887-6777.

First Voyager Books edition 2000
Voyager Books is a registered trademark of Harcourt, Inc.

The Library of Congress has cataloged the hardcover edition as follows:
Bunting, Eve.
Flower garden/Eve Bunting; illustrated by Kathryn Hewitt.
p. cm.
Summary: Helped by her father, a young girl prepares a
flower garden as a birthday surprise for her mother.
(1. Gardening—Fiction. 2. Parent and child—Fiction. 3. Birthdays—Fiction.
4. Stories in rhyme.) I. Hewitt, Kathryn, ill. II. Title.
PZ8.3.B92Fl 1994
(E)—dc20   92-25766
ISBN 0-15-228776-0

ISBN 0-15-202372-0 pb

E F D

Printed in Singapore

The paintings in this book were done in oil paint on paper.
The display type and text type were set in Benguiat
by Thompson Type, San Diego, California.
Color separations by Bright Arts, Ltd., Singapore
Printed and bound by Tien Wah Press, Singapore
This book was printed on Arctic matte paper.
Production supervision by Stanley Redfern and Pascha Gerlinger
Designed by Lisa Peters

For Anna Eve,
who makes beautiful flower gardens.

— E. B.

For Diane D'Andrade and Jeannette Larson,
who can turn dandelions into daffodils.

— K. H.

Garden in a shopping cart
Doesn't it look great?

Garden on the checkout stand
I can hardly wait.

Garden in a cardboard box
Walking to the bus

Garden sitting on our laps
People smile at us!

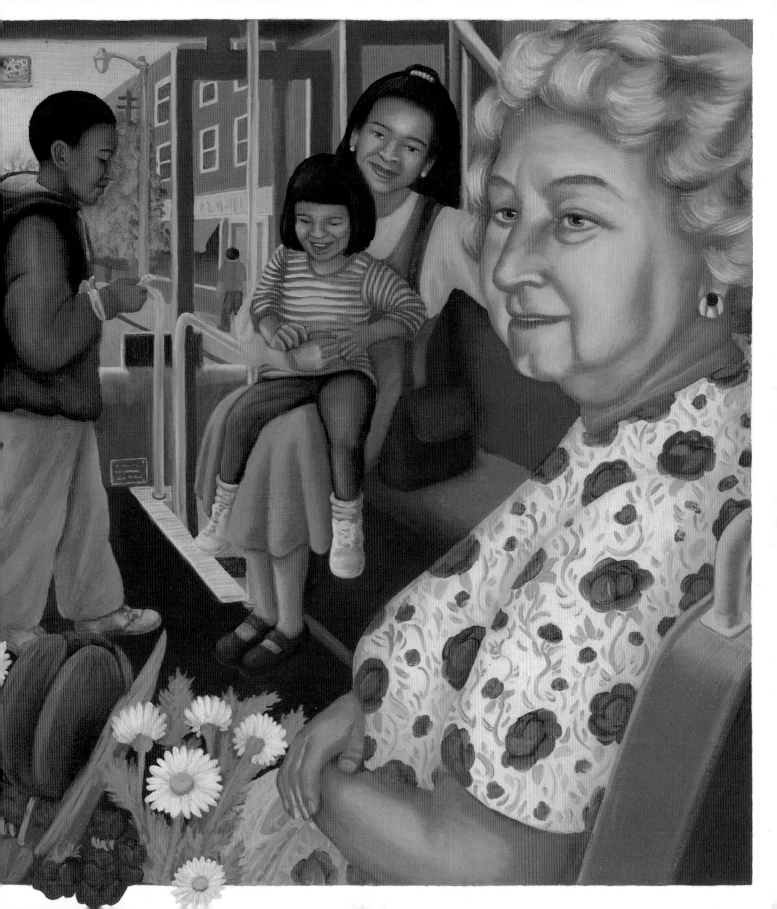

Garden going up the stairs
Stopping at each floor

This garden's getting heavier!
At last — our own front door.

Hurry! Hurry! Get the trowel
Spread the papers thick.

Get the bag of potting soil
Get the planting mix.

Put purple
pansies at
each end

Daisies, white
as snow

Daffodils, and tulips

geraniums in a row.

Garden in a window box
High above the street

Where butterflies
can stop and rest
And ladybugs can meet.

Walkers walking down below
Will lift their heads and see
Purple, yellow, red, and white
A color jamboree.

Candles on a birthday cake
Chocolate ice cream, too.

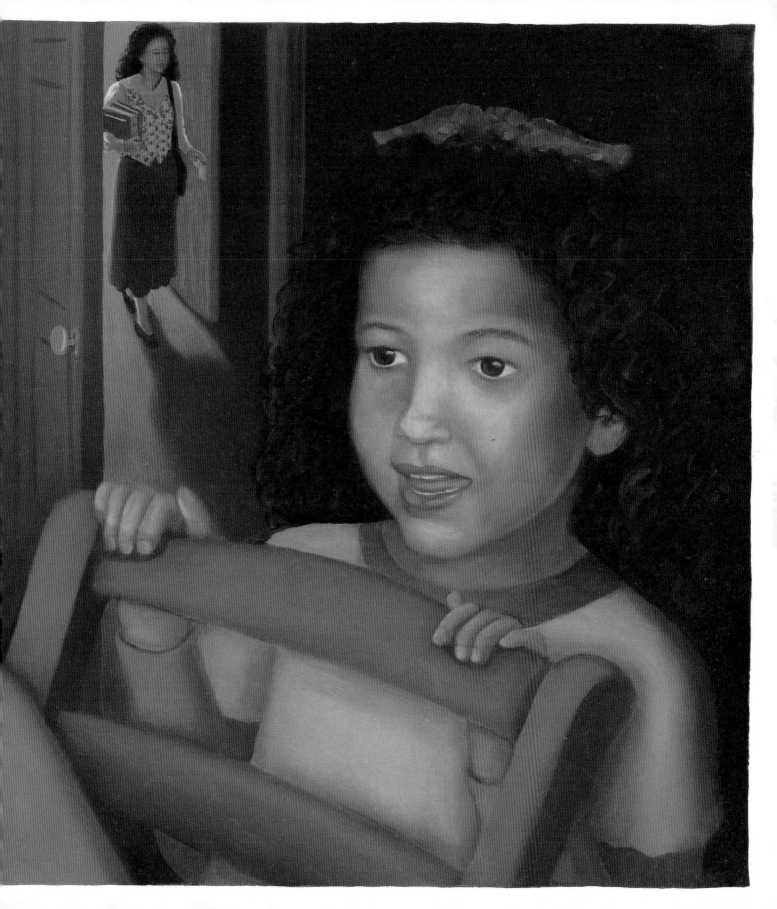

Happy, happy birthday, Mom!
A garden box — for you.